ZAK ◇
THE
ONE-OF-A-KIND
DOG

◇◇◇◇◇◇◇◇◇◇◇◇◇◇◇◇◇◇◇◇◇◇◇

Jane Lidz

HARRY N. ABRAMS, INC., PUBLISHERS

For Zak,

whose love and spirit showed me

we are all one of a kind,

yet we are all one

A portion of the royalties from the sale of this book will be donated to
organizations helping animals.

Editor: Harriet Whelchel
Designer: Dana Sloan

Library of Congress Catalog Card Number: 96–79284
ISBN 0–8109–3995–9

Published in 1997 by Harry N. Abrams, Incorporated, New York
A Times Mirror Company
All rights reserved. No part of the contents of this book may be
reproduced without the written permission of the publisher

First published in black-and-white in 1982 by A & W Publishers
under the title *One of a Kind*

Printed in Hong Kong

 Harry N. Abrams, Inc.
100 Fifth Avenue
New York, N.Y. 10011
www.abramsbooks.com

The first thing people ask me is,

"What kind of dog are you?"

I wish I knew. Someone said there were many
kinds of dogs in my family. Who were they?

Judge

Pirate

Trailblazer

Pioneer

Country Farmer

I'll have to seek the answer.

Excuse me, but . . .

Do you know what kind of dog I am?

Am I the top dog?

Or the underdog?

I'm not black or white.

I'm not even on the dog chart.

But, at least I'm a real dog...

with real feelings.

I can be brave

honest

funny

playful

curious

and loving.

There's no one else just like me.

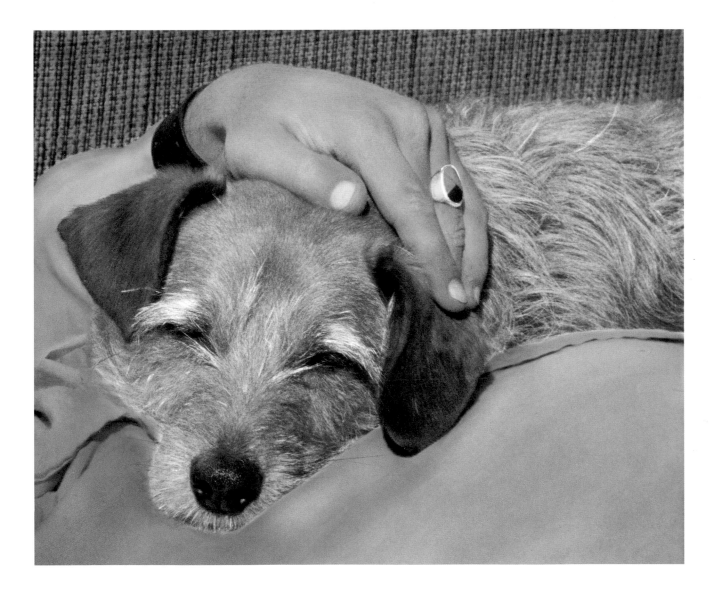

It feels good to be special.

Now when people ask, "What kind of dog are you?"

I say, "I'm a one-of-a-kind dog."

What kind of person are you?